*Prose, Photos
and Poems*

Prose, Photos and Poems

GEORGE G A WENSLEY

AuthorHouse™
1663 Liberty Drive
Bloomington, IN 47403
www.authorhouse.com
Phone: 1-800-839-8640

© 2012 by George G A Wensley. All rights reserved.

No part of this book may be reproduced, stored in a retrieval system, or transmitted by any means without the written permission of the author.

Published by AuthorHouse   11/20/2012

ISBN: 978-1-4772-4665-8 (sc)
ISBN: 978-1-4772-4668-9 (e)

Any people depicted in stock imagery provided by Thinkstock are models, and such images are being used for illustrative purposes only.
Certain stock imagery © Thinkstock.

This book is printed on acid-free paper.

Because of the dynamic nature of the Internet, any web addresses or links contained in this book may have changed since publication and may no longer be valid. The views expressed in this work are solely those of the author and do not necessarily reflect the views of the publisher, and the publisher hereby disclaims any responsibility for them.

Contents

Red Ken's Pipe 1
Plagiarism 5
Slick 8
Splash 10
What's in a look? 12
Valentine's Day 14
The Dreamlands 20
Broadstairs 27
Ramsgate 31
The Lexicographers 33
Madam Cliché 35
Venice in the rain 38
Venice 43
Fruit de Mare at Mira Mere 44
Waiting for the train 50
Dreamlands Post Script 54
A tale of two book signings 56

Red Ken's Pipe

It was his habit when walking into town, looking for his favourite coffee shop, to walk to a weir, in the hinterland of the local park. One moment he was avoiding cars, the next he was on a tarmacked path with trees and grass. In front of him was an old woman with wrinkled plastic bags that were laden with precious bric-a-brac, with two dogs lying down. She fed pigeons while muttering either to her dogs, the pigeons or some unknown entity.

The man had lived in the country where the sight of a pigeon would have brought out shot guns and cob pie that would have been on the menu that day.

Then after a few paces he was at the weir. The water fell over the lip, mesmerizing; it was not constant like a watch, with the seasons it changed from muddy murk to crystal clear and from rushed spate to lazy warmth. The weir was made of red brick, which was worn by the water and water borne debris, tennis balls from the tennis courts, footballs, tin cans, bottles and wood. It was the wood that fascinated him, the most; the back draft of the weir tumbled all of these items, like a maelstrom turned in ninety degrees became rounded and smooth, where they constantly hit the abrasive bricks. He had worked in a factory where there was a machine that did exactly this for metal pieces. He remembered something that was of utmost beauty to him. A log with ivy smothering the bark, it too tumbled in the water, but the branches of ivy remained in skeletal white over the red log, in a natural sculpture.

Today the water was, a clear green, striating the red bricks as it fell. In the turmoil at the bottom of the weir, was a football, two tennis balls, a corked bottle of wine and the usual tumbled pieces of wood. His next habit was to chuck an imaginary Pooh stick into the water and walk to the other side of the bridge.

Here the water eddied in a normal way for river water. Across the river were pipes some small in diameter, some big in diameter. The largest one was the one that he had named 'Red Ken's Pipe.' A pigeon spread its wings in a braking, turning and loosing height action to land on the pipe. It wasn't the first pigeon to do this as there were heaps of pigeon shit on the pipe. They always landed on this pipe. The pigeons reminded him of Ken Livingstone and this was why he called it 'Red Ken's Pipe.' The man had once known Red Ken's PA, when Red Ken was Mayor of London, when he, the man, lived in Rochester; the PA was a perfect paralysing blond. These recollections triggered flashes of memory, the bullet hit the mirror of the present, and he was back in the past, The Nag's Head that had a parrot and an artistic punk band. Other memories intrude like seeing brilliant white gulls seen through the net curtains of a hotel room, the white bird dazzling in sunlight and blue skies. These memories tumbled into, the mewing of sea gulls, dropped ice cream cones, fish and chips and the ozone smell of rotting sea weed. In the room that had a sea gull hanging over it, there was a notice with the legend, 'Keep the windows shut to keep out the pigeons.' On the ledge outside were spiked defences against pigeons. He remembered Ken's statement "pigeons are rats with wings."

Another pigeon lands on the pipe. Even if you love or hate pigeons, you cannot fail to be mesmerised by their court-ship dance, like something from 'Strictly Come Dancing' they strut their Tango. The bloke pigeon's head going forward asking the question then retreating, the chick pigeon preened in a fashionable way refuses at first and then they dance.

Then an interloper lands and tries to muscle in, the two bloke pigeons cross their bills, wings flutter, claws gouge and feathers fly. The intruder backs off and flies away, while he still has feathers.

The love pigeons resume their courtship, the chick excited by the success of the victor. The bloke pigeon mounts; a quick rub of the bill against the neck, a flutter of the wings and the genetic urge is satisfied.

Or as Red Ken might say, "look at those fucking pigeons, it costs the council millions to clean up their shit."

These intercourses of the memory and the present, jangle in the man's head. He needs that coffee, but no toffee cake. The birds have flown, and so must he.

He trudges down a dark alley, a few steps away, from the managed green grass of the park, and then he's on the High Street. It is busy with cars, owned by people that can barely afford them, this fact showing on their faces, on the street more people spending time and money they haven't got. He turned right and into his haven the coffee shop. The smell of freshly roasted coffee that he recalled from his boyhood eluded him except in his memory, because this would be his third coffee.

The coffee shop, his haven, was bright, painted Italian blue, with pictures of men that had time to play cards; he wandered which game, Gin Rummy? There was another cloth picture of women chatting over coffee on the wall and at tables.

The man stood in line.

"What would you like today, the usual, Sir? And to eat we have muffins and cookies?"

Was he tempted? He looked into her eyes, he was getting fat, and she wanted more money for the till. Then there was that dilemma between pleasure and cost.

"As it is morning," her eyes lit up, "I will have an apricot-"

A man behind him in the queue interrupted, frustration was swooping in his eyes. "I'm in a hurry."

With a frosty calm the man with blue eyes gazed at the interloper, and thought of the sparing pigeons. They gazed into each-other's eyes wandering weather to cross swords, the interlopers eyes flew away in resignation.

The smile and warmth returned. "As I was saying, as it is morning I will have an Apricot Croissant with my coffee."

He took his goods, sat down, added sweetener, and had that first bite of croissant and that first sip of coffee.

Plagiarism

"Docket number two, three, three, three, Collins versus A. U. Thor, plagiarism," the clerk of the court read.

"This is a clear case of plagiarism," said the offence lawyer, dressed in a white suit and white wig that contrasted with her brown doe like eyes and dark brown hair.

The defence lawyer, dressed in a black suit and stockings and a wig that barely contained her full blond hair interrupted, "I object your honour! My client is just using the words in Collin's publication and re-arranging them so they portray a different feel and meaning. Yes my client is using the words in the book. In fact all his words are in Collins's-"

"Over rule your honour. The honourable lady's client, has on occasion sat at his computer and read my client's book, then uses the words-"

"Rubbish your honour. He is just checking spe-"

"Order, order and I say again ORDER! I find this case tenuous. How do we define plagiarism?"

The offensive and defensive lawyers speak at the same time. The offensive lawyer says. "Plagiarism is where an individual-"

The defensive lawyer says. "Plagiarism is where-"

The descant was not harmonious.

The judge gets confused and annoyed, which wasn't a difficult task. "Order, order, and I say ORDER! One at a time gentle people, please can I have the defensive lawyer first, speak but don't bellow."

"Plagiarism is where an author copies word for word a textual string of words from one book to another. It is a heinous crime. There are two prongs to his defence. We have reviews on file of critiques which state and I quote, 'Mr Thor as being un-readable, not worthy of being called an author, and' (this is their pun not mine) 'not God like at all.'"

"You may proceed with the defence," said the Judge, dressed in a dark gown and white wig.

The defensive lawyer bristles. "Although my client on these occasions; is sat at his computer and has his Collin's Dictionary open, and I stress this, copies letter for letter words into his books; not, I repeat, not strings of words from the publication Collins Dictionary. I further-"

The judge interrupts through boredom and misplaced fairness to the offensive lawyer. "You've had your say councillor; it is now the turn of the offence."

"I was just getting to the interesting-"

"Enough! Precede offensive councillor."

"My learned colleague has stated the law correctly, but interpreted it in-correctly."

"I object."

"I don't recall the offensive councillor interrupting you. Please continue offensive council."

"Further-more in the defendant's publication, 'Dane Law' he writes and I quote, 'the definition of plague quoting Colin's Dictionary is a virulent contagious bacterial disease.' That according to the defence is a string of words."

The court room fell to stunned silence. A. U. Thor looked at the floor then his councillor. Who put her hands on her hips and raised an eye brow, she sat, raised a finger and beckoned her client, and a whispered intercourse ensued.

The defence counsellor stood up. "My client wishes to change his plea to guilty."

Guilty reverberated around the court room and the judge felt he needed to use his gavel. "All rise. The defendant is found to be guilty sentencing to be on the sixteenth of December."

"Docket number two, three, three, and four . . ."

Slick

There was a nick to my throat. Why had I chosen this barber? Why did I want my hair cut and a shave? Why a shave? Was it old hat, to have a shave, in the twenty first century, or chic retro style?

I suppose the place looked interesting, there was stubble on my chin, and I was looking for a comb, and I needed to get out of the piercing morning Sun.

The place looked Sicilian, in a nice way, nothing heavy, nothing would go down, but I would get the sense of fear.

So I needed a number four with a number two at the sides. The sun was bright, the sky was blue, and why did I go into that barber's shop.

The place smelt of man perfume. There was a queue. I put the hat and coat on the rack, sat down on the red plastic sofa bench, in front of the table with soft porn of the auto kind, soft porn of the football kind and soft porn of the female kind. It didn't grab me, but a picture on the wall did.

It was the head of a horse, its long tongue lolled from its mouth, protruding from its death mask gaze, there were no taught veins, and it was as if the blood had been drained from it. This was unsettling.

Blood oozed from the nick and dribbled on to the apron and formed a blood slick on it.

Next to the horse a picture of Etna erupting, blood red lines punctuating a dark mountain and sky. I should have known it was no wise crack.

Next to the volcano was a picture of a slick haired man, this is what you would look like if you walked from the barbers shop.

The barber seemed happy, as he stropped the cut throat razor on the leather strap. Rasp, rasp like a last gasp.

Soon it was my turn. Smiling didn't seem like the appropriate manner. I sat. The apron was swirled around me. On the counter was a stainless steel tank for the hot wet towels, it fumed like Etna and an espresso machine.

The glasses came off. The banter began, the order given. Did I say something wrong again?

Shave first, the nick, the slick and then the hot towel; darkness.

"Sorry Sir. I have plaster."

Splash

The latte splashed.

Yesterday I was at the coffee shop Nero's, where I saw a man spill his coffee, but there was a sequence of events that led up to this incident, which revealed much about the man and brought back memories for me.

I was sitting in the shop near the plate glass windows that over looked the square. Outside under the awning were aluminium seats and tables for smokers. He was a large man with a beard, he had warm clothes on. It was sunny, but it was a typical English autumn morning, damp chill, with mist hindering the sun's path to the ground. The damp moistened the leaves on the trees and those lying on the ground, where the trees, being serial litter bugs had dropped them, for the environment department to blow them away.

But; in the coffee shop the sky was blue. I only noticed the man because, he either brushed or used for support a fold up sign, on the brick block pavement. It, the board, did the splits and fell to the floor. Amazingly, he didn't at that point spill his coffee. It did make him agitated though, and he looked as if he needed that latte. In his shock and tiredness, he went to his seat, tried to put down the coffee, and in his agitation finally spilt the coffee, then put it on the table. Now, this is the important point, I noticed that he had a bandage on his carrying hand. That brought back memories for me, nursing wounds and always trying to shield them from pain, then hitting the wound and it hurting, which led to mistakes. He was good though; he smiled and got through it.

I knew where he was, though.

What's in a look?

We look across a sea of people searching for answers.

What's in that look? Is it a serious look or a smile?

I look for hidden meanings, that I don't understand,

And read what I want into them

    I read love when it is admiration

Love is what I'm searching for

But I should be searching for friendship

What does love mean? What does friendship mean?

The kind of love that leads to tactile passion,

The kind of love that says, kind of, I don't want to be alone.

The kind of love that should be friendship but hurts

Emotions jangle and he is laid bare

    Then there is that look that hurts him the most and says,

    I want you to be happy but not with me, a smiling expression,

    One desperate not to hurt, one desperate not to be hurt

    One understanding, one not; one living with loneliness

    One just coming to understanding it

Knowing and not knowing have equal pain,

She is hiding in her work,

He is trying not to hide.

She is clothed in her emotions,

He is laid bare by them, both knowing that

A simple friendship and a smile will do.

Or is that an obsessive hope, that should be let go of?

But still, what's in a look?

Valentine's Day

I continue with my love affair with words, the day goes in a blur, it is almost physical, and I hope fiscal I pause to

Eat, to drink, to breathe, I struggle with the flow to keep the precious momentum and have no breaks in the

Reader's quest for the next page,

My writing animates,

Bringing me to life

I hunger for a pleasant meal and company who speak my language and like what I like

It is dysfunctional papers everywhere. I must stop I must go to poetry class

I surface and go through the ritual for the outside world taking the
feral me off

Then pick up the past poems that I have let die in my mind like
embers in a fire

It is only possible to breathe new life into them while they are
dormant

I go to the coffee shop; the girls know that I am writing a thriller

It is dangerous each wants to be the lead character

They smile at me vying to be the lead character

Who should I choose?

There is no poker game in the back of a legit

Garage no tommy guns rat a tat tatting No massacre

No cards given or received no pain, no giving my all

In words to a card no loss no gain

Rhyme and Madrigal used to rule so the free poets

Had to destroy that language in its imperial beauty then

To their horror or joy they became the establishment about to fall

More people hating English But using it like a drug they cannot
put down

They subvert it writing prose poems I cannot hide from what I feel

I cannot accept the truth   I must be tolerant

The soldier must wait   in line to be spat

At to be shot at but   he survives

Another look   that says I wish

Him well   smile No loss,

No gain,   no shame

Just me   and my

Love affair   with words

Some one's in trouble. A Pythagoras Poem, A squared plus B squared equals C squared 12:16:20
12x12
The dog hunt
For the cat
Whom chasers
The mouse to
Catch and to
Torment then
Make it feel
So bad it is
Helpless and
Without help
Then go with
Hate an' kill
16x16
The rat must run

Quick or he will
Be caught a claw
At a time in the
Cat's game of get
Caught get out A
Rest Get a timed
Reprieve For cat
To chase again
Strand of terror
Never seeming to
End then the dog
Sees the cat and
Gets mad with it
The cat gets her
Chance and flees
20x20
Cat on the hot roofs
Rat runs away and to
Stop its fear it eat
Fish and not chips A
Chance to run faster
A pitta for the rat
To patter in smatter
And batter a tempter
A prelude a disaster
Grated rat the cat a
Nine tails licks its
Lips slurps the last
Part of rat's tail to

Smudge lick away the
Blood and is rest at
Ease When dog sees a
Cat, The cat see the
Dog's tail then turn
And run through rails
Of a fence Dog stuck

The Dreamlands

Margate

There was a compulsion to go to the Turner exhibition at Margate. Moreover he felt duty bound to go, as Margate was the victim of market forces. The thought reverberates through his soul, 'economics can be as devastating as all-out war.'

The high speed train draws into Margate. It travels past a scaffold clad roller coaster, looking as if it were a parcel ready for despatch to its last resting place, rather than refurbishment. The roller coaster used to be a big draw in the sixties and seventies, owned by the town until it was sold out to a person that promised money, but had none to give.

Prose, Photos and Poems

A grey light preluding snow evaded warmth, as the writer alights at the station. He plods past the coffee shop wanting to give a little business to the town. There is a lot of work being done on the town; white granite is every-where, the granite is the paving for the walkways, it provides places to sit, and places to eat take away food.

His plan was to walk along the Esplanade, where the road, the deity of automobiles, is busy, he crosses at a pelican crossing, wanting to grab a coffee at a café, that sat on the sands like a beached whale, but the cafe was boarded up, closed for the season, and looking like a set for a sit com, where none of the characters laugh.

That café was his first port of call on the opening day of the Turner gallery, a bacon sandwich and a black coffee. Blue skies a sandy beach that had been cleaned and preened a thousand times, in preparation for the opening of the Turner Gallery. Now the roller shutters were down.

Margate had the auto-mobile bug. There was work being done ahead, you mustn't disturb the cars, vans and Lorries; so pedestrians had to cross the road, away from the health giving shore line. He crossed and he had to walk past a nightclub, where you had to wear tops, but there was no mention of bottoms though. This was a sad haven as the other shops were shut, part of the economic nemesis.

There was a whole covered arcade without a single shop open, not even a charity shop. It was the entrance to Dreamlands. *Did Margate dream of its past?* If it did, was it going to be a long haul, to regain it?

A cold east wind blew a multi pack bag up, and it drifted aimlessly to the ground waiting for the next injection of breeze to raise it to the skies, its presence intruding the greyness like a bad memory, or a dazzling light.

Where had all the coffee shops gone? How can he help a town that dreams of its past, if there is nowhere for a coffee? Then, around a corner, there is an oasis of commerce, a coffee shop that looked like a pub. A buzz on the door, a cuddly local accent, half full with customers. He had given up asking for a small cup of coffee anywhere, so he asked for a regular Americano and no milk. There was small happy talk, his Americano and a bacon sandwich. He wondered what Dell and Rodney would say, about a pub made into a coffee shop? They had made it, and stopped going to Margate, even though they had scattered Granddad's Ashes off the end of the Pier.

He, the man, would go to the end of the stone pier. The writer gazed at the machinery on top of it, he thought about the risks that must have been taken by the builders and the lives lost because of the need to protect lives at sea, for work and sustanence, the builders needed to get away from London and its lack of sanitation, its cholera, the green disease and its hopelessness, desperate measures. They brought the problems of London with them, so they were a mixed blessing, a bounty that had a price, their price.

He felt drawn to the pier, the last time he was here was at the opening of Turner Gallery, and he waited at the end of the pier with a coffee, for the opening of the gallery. Where there were bright search lights, pointing into the harbour in brilliant day light, paid for by an Arts Council grant. *Very conceptual* he thought the amount had no meaning, and there was no practical point to it, but he liked it, and that's what art should do: be liked, after a process of shock. The search lights were making a point, in their pointless way, one fired its light like a cannon bouncing its ball over the waves, and the other enfiladed the harbour, up lighting the sea wall with shimmering water reflections, your money (already granted) or your art.

The man put his fleece cap on, was that a chink of blue in the sky? A short walk to the end of the pier: there were some businesses that were open, and were about to open, to capture the bounty brought by the Turner Gallery. Where he should have crossed the busy esplanade, to go along the pier to the end, where he had waited for the Turner Gallery to open with a coffee or two, and listened to Tracy Em's opening speech. Tracy who brought back memories of Rochester, he had not known her, but she was there in the mid-eighties, she had played for a band in the Nags Head with a parrot caged on the bar. Such an artist, famous for her 'bed without a name' with delicate arrangement of condoms on an untidy bed, which symbolised life at that time, like the search lights the art focused on the present and was sold for a commercially absurd amount, but there was 'loads of money' then, the bed had an artistic pointlessness like 'I don't like Mondays.' Tracy grew up in Margate, it was the place that influenced her the most, she dreamed that Margate would re-birth itself with the Turner Gallery, the passion resonated through her voice and words, it was her dreamland and not to be a wasteland. Joules Holland was there as well, a local talent, but for how much longer? Was his castle going to be an airport hub or a runway? A group of school children did a performance as Vikings. It got close to the opening time. The writer joined the orderly crowd as it was ushered, with shuffling feet, along a confined walkway; there were photographers sniping photos, news teams rolling their cameras to record the event for posterity. Shuffle, rest, and shuffle and . . . It was not a dance to induce endorphins, although there was excitement at getting to the gallery. The event was about the opening, not the gallery. There was a big crisis between having a lot of people attending the event and seeing the art. His father had taught him to focus on one or two pieces of art, stand back till you saw the picture and not the brush strokes; the writer enjoyed Sister Wendy's discourses on art. And others who described the perspectives, how the artist drew the eye in, with an old imagery; this is impossible with large crowds.

There was a shop, a large clear donation box, and a crowded foyer. He had walked up the concrete stairs; poetry adorned the steps in a large Arial font.

He had wanted to go to the end of the pier, but it was being refurbished, another disappointment. The recollections and aspirations went to naught. So he walked up the main steps, the cold weather making it stark and denuded of people. He walked to the reception area and put a piece of paper into the donation box, got a program browsed, but didn't buy from the shop. He went to the stairs, the poetry had gone but there was a patina beginning to appear on the concrete moulded hand rail. He loved patina, a product of watching too many antique shows, the love of oils to the touch and the contact with so many un-seen people.

It was good to look at the pictures and not be huddled up next to other art goers. He loved Turner because from a very early age he had gone to Ramsgate every month, one of the things that he loved, when returning home in the evening were the sun sets, the dramatic red and blue painted skies and Turner did dramatic sun sets so well.

He had seen many of the pictures before, but he never tired of them, some were experimental mere wash on paper with delicate un-assuming detail, some were very complicated and elemental, which was the theme of the exhibition. The writer loved the fact that Turner messed with perspective, or more precisely he changed the vanishing points, the norm being one on the left side of the picture, one on the right and the focus for the picture being in the centre. Turner learned to make the vanishing point in the centre of the picture, the perspective lines radiating out from this point. This was particularly effective in his stormy elemental seascapes. There was even one picture where there were two epicentres one dark and one light, this was the painting that the writer loved the most. He loved the fact that Turner was able to do this without being distracted by digital paint boxes, pop ups and fire walls, the fact that the painter only had his surface to paint on, his paints, and the many hours that he just sat and observed water.

It was time to go. The writer descended the stairs, adding to the patina on the concrete moulded hand rail.

Outside on the raised platform he took pictures with his reflex digital camera, it was the way he worked, he seldom if ever took pictures of people, but he loved taking landscape photos. He took a picture of Margate Sands from the south of platform taking in the coffee shop he had used, and then he took the picture from the north of the platform. Next to the platform was a cafeteria where he noticed people looking at him. He didn't use a tri-pod that was too techno and pernickety for him, he hoped he looked like a gifted dilettante, but guessed that they were saying 'he can take the cold, sooner him than me, it looks freezing out there!' Whatever, he blanked their voices and their looks from his mind and continued taking shots.

His desire for photography sated, he wound the windy path back to the station, crossing the road several times, past the economic fall out of the arcade, which because of the poor light was coquettish about being photographed, but he stood there and looked at an empty space that was once full of life, it was under reconstruction. Would the dreams of Dreamland re-appear?

Broadstairs

He didn't have to wait long for the train. On his last visit to Margate he had thought it a good idea to walk to Broadstairs along the coast, as it only took five minutes by train. It was a good walk but it took ages to get to Broadstairs, so today he went by train, past the scaffold-clad roller coaster.

It had been a sunny may day; the surface of the sea wall was flat, but seemed to go on for ever. He past sea adventure centres with jet boats zooming about on the water. Again it took him a long time to reach a place that did any sort of food. The cliffs, because the tides built up here, had green algae at the bottom of them, looking like green socks. There was a gap in the cliffs with a walk way that according to local lore was cut by smugglers.

Out-side of the café he saw people dinking in the winter sun shine with their eyes closed and faces turned to the brief warmth of the sun. He had a coffee and a bacon sandwich which was bliss. Then continued to Broadstairs where he caught the train home. Broadstairs was a place that was very familiar to him from an early age. It was a place that he never tired of. There was a set itinerary, off the platform, over the railway bridge, down onto the High Street. Then to the cliffs edge esplanade, down to the scooped out harbour protected by a broad pier with a large roofed area that housed stalls for ice cream and sea food, he remembered seeing in a gale, a wave hitting the sea wall then spuming over the top of the roofed pier. It was not like that today; was that blue in the sky? It warmed his soul after being in the miasma of Margate. He walked around the pier, then back up the arched road to the esplanade and Morelli's, an Italian coffee and gelato shop. It had been there since the start of the twentieth century, started by immigrants from an outer Venetian island.

As a child the writer with his family had walked from the East Cliff at Ramsgate, come the rain, come shine, in winter the walk was always bracing. This was known territory.

He sat in Morelli's, the décor and furnishings hadn't been changed in decades and he found that most reassuring, and had a coffee, the past and present recollections meandering together to form a sense of wellbeing. A sense of sameness, which was strange as the coffee and gelato emporium was built on a chalk cliff, and that rock is easy to mould. Like Turner he sat on a seat looking at the ever changing sea. It was calm now but that didn't mean that a wind could blow up and drive waves to the bottom of the unprotected cliffs to undercut them and cause a chalk fall.

Sea walls were an ancient edifice built by dark-age monks to re-claim land from the sea and ward off Viking raiders. Thanet had been an island until the sea wall went from Reculver to Birchington and drained the marshes to make new lands. This brought prosperity, but to the west it also brought mosquitos, which brought ague, which brought death and named the town Gravesend.

Two mothers walked into Morelli's, complete with child buggies, a piece of machinery that always intimidated the writer, extruded tubes bolted together with unions, large wheels with soft tyres, a place to put the shopping, a place to put the mobile phone, always empty, cigarettes, lighter, and, not to be forgotten, a space for a small child. They chose a table, sat older children down, who immediately got up and ran around. "I'm warning you." The mothers obviously needed a well-earned rest from the stress of using the mobile phone. It was time to go.

Another of his rituals when in Broadstairs was to go to a small art gallery, set back off the road running parallel to the Esplanade. A half glazed door with crown glass and a bell which had been modernised to a buzzer. It was the show case of a local artist, there was a sale on and he knew that he would buy something. There were panoramic pictures of Broadstairs from the sea or the pier. Still life's, pictures of children on a sandy beach, the back room had more exotic pictures of London in the rain, Paris and women posed to attract. 'One day' he thought. At the back, was a picture framing workshop. He returned to the front of the shop. It had always been an ambition to get a cat, and there was a picture of several of them for only £7.50 there were several cats all with different catty expressions, some were aloof barely purring, some had deep soulful eyes saying. 'Feed me you dumb human.' Some were huntresses, but all had beguiling eyes. This was the picture, he chatted to the woman in charge. He always shopped here, that was good, she liked cats as well, he promoted his book, and he even smiled as he punched in his pin number.

When he exited there was brilliant sunshine, the sea was as blue as the sky. He past the old boarding house where Dickens had stayed, he was still selling books, and the writer bemoaned the fact that it was the 200th birthday of Charles Dickens; he called this 'un-dead writing.' He moved swiftly on, past the band stand that had featured in so many TV adverts, then down to a cut in the cliffs.

The sun was bright, but the wind was cold.

He went down some steps, thirty nine in all, to the concrete sea wall underneath the cliffs. The wall that faced the sea was curved upwards to deflect waves that wanted to penetrate the land. Beneath the wall were green algae covered steps that merged into a sandy beach, then into the foreground was a sea weed and mussel covered chalk pavement.

Ramsgate

It was the home straight now. The cliffs rose from the wall, and were whiter than the cliffs of Dover, except for near the top, where there was a foot of brown soil. With the sun his mood changed, there was a spring in his step, a sense of great expectations. Women walked their dogs on the beach, on the water solidified sand, chucking balls with their ball throwing devices. He waved to one or two of them. One of his anticipations was to have a coffee at the Dumpton Gap Kiosk. He rounded a corner and got eye contact with the kiosk, there were no tables or chairs next to the edge of the wall, and the shutters were down.

The sea wall ended here. The tide was out, so he wouldn't have to climb the cut and walk on the top of the cliffs. When he put his foot on the sand it was on the cusp of being dry, it then half sank, half crunched, as he walked along.

Then he was at the remains of the Ramsgate lido. It was a car park now, but in the eighties it was a night club called Caesars. The sea defence held a wide piece of land, where houses were dug into the face of the cliff. At one time there was a static air ground, nothing as big as Dreamlands but it had dodgems, a helter-skelter, other rides and the obligatory Bingo emporium. These were memories, boarded up with art work about Ramsgate, each board done by a different artist and or organisation in the town. Like Turner's paintings they had empathy for their locality and held recollections like water. The art wall ended, and he stood in a plaza. He stood on the site of a Wimpy Kiosk, but he didn't think 'Time Team' would excavate it.

He looked at an amusement arcade that still existed.

Then a famous fish and chips shop.

The blond curls 'Hi there.'

'Hi there' he said.

She faded like

Dreamlands

The Lexicographers

They all wore the same clothes, even the bloke in the back seat. They were neatly dressed. Razors had caressed their chins. The same jeans covered their pins, the same hooded sweat shirts.

"This is sweet."

Emotions were high the buzz was nigh.

"Where's the heat?"

"What?"

"That's assonance."

"You nonce, what the fuck is assonance."

"I did literature in the choky, it was a cure, anything to pass the time and get out faster. Let me illiterate assonance is where two words sound the same and are used close together, like crows and crap."

The one in the back seat fingered the money. Would his misses moan and hiss when he put the money on the table?

Blue lights in the rear view mirror. The driver floored the accelerator. "Let's get our assonances out of here!"

Word count 142

Madam Cliché

Madam Cliché sits in her Hackney cab, waiting for her journey to end.

She wears a little black dress.

The blemishes from her skin have been covered by makeup.

Like an airbrush on a photo.

She crosses her legs and wonders if she really is beautiful.

Madam Cliché is going from one event to another.

The smile is constant but it has no wonder and doesn't reach the eyes

Madam Cliché's body is traveling, but she isn't

The body is traveling in a fashion, or with a fleeting fashion

From one event to the next

The clichés are hiding her

The psyche is hidden, the smile never changes

Madam Cliché's soul festers

Hidden behind the shows and the imagery

Madam Cliché knows

Where her body is going

But her soul doesn't

Madam needs her clichés

Or she would be naked

Even then, would her soul breathe?

Madam Cliché sells what

She knows,

She lives by her clichés

A text, her soul and eyes light up

The next piece of busyness

The next event

Was her soul that shallow?

Madam Cliché arrives

The world turns its head

The world looks at the image

But can't fathom the soul,

And the eye's cease to breath.

Venice in the rain

When going to Venice, you don't expect to see the rain. It is different to English rain, it is warm, in England it has a cold bite to it, and the rain also comes with an energy sapping wind.

In Venice the rain falls softly, to me it is warm, I wear a T shirt but my fellow tourists wear red cagoules with 'I love Venice' on them, except the love is a picture of a heart. The locals wear stylish leather jackets or woollies with jeans.

Early on Sunday Venice is waking up, the streets are almost empty. I have an espresso and croissant in an oriental bar. I'm surprised to hear the Orientals speaking Italian to each other.

I walk through the Piazza San Marco and to the broad walkway next to the 'Canal di San Marco.' Where a cruise liner is being pulled into dock, one tug is pulling the liner; another is at the stern keeping the ship in line.

It is cloudy perhaps the sun will burn off the clouds. No such luck. I'm nearing a public park and it starts raining. Is it raining in Venice?

The rain is warm, a blessing from the skies. Light reflects, as if, on a pool, off of the stone paving. With the rain the ochre on the walls gets darker, less washed out. When the rain gets hard I dip into cafes and have espressos or soda lemon. It is showers not rain though.

Thank god for rain, I'm not bored! It is always a good ice breaker in conversation.

As I stroll through Venice's streets I wonder if this is what a Roman city must have been like. I have seen a documentary about Rome on the TV; it describes Rome and its suburbia, and tall buildings with narrow walkways. The colour of the water on canals is dark Italian blue.

Miramar near to Trieste

I saw my first gecko today in an ornamental garden of the castle Miramar.

As you can see the camouflage is superb. The garden was formal and I recognised many of the plants. The gecko was investigating a box hedge. To it, the gecko, the hedge must have been like an impenetrable forest. To me it was small. In the centre of the forest was a glade of pansies. The tulips were going to seed. It seemed that the plants were being taken for granted, but they just grow here. In Britain it is a life and death scenario for plants that like warmth. I had an Espresso by the harbour, my Italian is poor and I only had twenty Euros' so I had to have a croissant. There were several herbs growing in jardinières, rosemary, Basle and thyme.

There is another Gecko siting over there, she looks Italian, dark hair with a hint of auburn in it, a black cardigan, a long dress white with hoops, sunglasses and a very large husband, it is only now that I notice the child's buggy. Time to go!

*

I sit in the shade of an awning, in a café next to a lido, chaise longs on concrete, with blocks of rough lime stone set in it. A palm type of plant in a plastic pot the colour of sun tanned bathers, and was that an olive bush wrapped in yellow plastic and ribbons.

La mere is blue, buoys lean in the current. La mere is flat.

Can I see Croatia? A dark wooded landscape with mist and smoke drifting from it.

There are in front of me two Italian women, wearing bikinis and had tans that were definitely not sprayed on or acquired on a sun bed, but I suppose the loungers may cost the same as a tanning session.

The coast road twinkles with traffic; the noise of tyres on tarmac invades the peace, Italian musing.

A sail boat motors into the wind.

*

Sun bathers lie on the concrete, all shapes, sizes and the occasional topless woman.

Venice

A sense of a lost dimension, you either stare up or down, narrow streets, per Rialto, per S. Marco. It is easy to get lost, but it is small. It is full of contradictions. You reach the Rialto cross it and find you are going the wrong way. I say this to the Major D at my hotel in front of his pigeon holes with their electronic keys; he says, "That's normal, even we Venetians get lost."

I like the plumbing in the hotel room, sophisticated but recognisable as taps hot and cold, you don't need a degree in design to understand them, which is bliss. In Venice I didn't use the air con, it was warm but the soft drinks were nice from the mini bar.

*

Ashford International, I do love traveling, everything is OK I'm on time and have my first espresso. The Eurostar train is good, the build is excellent. For so many years I have wanted to go on this train, when it went past where I used to work. All the bridges on the line had to be raised so it could get to Waterloo International. The first trains didn't supress the intense radio wave power of the engines, which used to corrupt the electronic control cards of our machines, but they sorted it out. I have a coffee, such sophistication, such power, but they only have one machine to heat the water!

Fruit de Mare at Mira Mere

The food is perfecto. Tonight I had spaghetti that looked like thin tagliatelle with prawns, tomatoes, garlic and basil, perfecto with mango sorbet which they call tropical, and an espresso to finish.

*

Today I go to Trieste to see the statue of James Joyce.

*

I had my fruit cocktail, and then I thought I had cracked the problem of cheese, ham and salami. What do you eat with it? I have tried the croissant, but that wasn't quite right. Today I saw the small excellent rolls; I thought I had cracked the problem. There was one small problem though, where was the butter? There was a squidgy parcel that I took to be a spread, I've cracked it! Much to my surprise when I got to my table and opened the parcel I found that it was cheese!

Now back to the Pizzeria at G Harbour. I'm waiting for the bus and have only a twenty Euro note and want a coffee, the woman asked me if I wanted a brioche. I communicate no but that I would like a croissant instead, I rub my stomach regretfully, there is a choice of course, chocolate or Marmalade. In England I have apricot croissant. I choose the marmalade.

*

When I arrived in Paris I was hungry and looked for something to eat immediately I left the Gare du Nord, and I was hit by the aroma of the East, namely spices. I found a shop with Samosas and sausages covered with bread. An Indian sat opposite me his English was good, he was apparently in the French army. I resisted the temptation to ask if he was in the Foreign Legion.

I went back to the Gare du Nord and caught the Double decker train to the Gare du Lion. I have my first espresso in France, and then it is walking about the station for a few hours for my train to Venice.

The monitor for departures is my sole amusement, apart from the very impressive trains that I see patiently waiting for their passengers to board and go to Bordeaux, Toulouse *et* all. It took a long time and much walking before Venice *Santa Lucia* to appear on the monitor, let alone the platform number, but the old enemy of time did pass, after much more walking, looking for a seat and walking.

Then to my relief a platform number was given. I wondered what it would be like to go on one off these Grand trains. My train was on the last platform, I rounded one of the inviting trains and for the first time saw my train, which was vintage 1960s or 70s. I couldn't put a price on it, but I definitely felt it was old enough to be auctioned off. Unfortunately there were no other platforms so I could not go to an upright, head but it, and get transported to a magical train, that would take me back to school.

The couchette was nice and crowded with young women. There was a conversation in one of the many languages that I don't fully understand. I don't let this bother me as it makes them feel safe. Then I'm asked if I would swap places with a young woman in the next compartment, I agree. In there I find a young family, mother, father and a bambino girl. It turns out that they are from Argentina. When I find this out I look out of the window and remember thirty years ago the home coming of our troops and naval vessels bound for Portsmouth Harbour, in hastily repaired and pockmarked ships. I remember the graves, more of them than us, I remember the men who relive the violent events in the Falklands, Mal Vinos, sour grapes indeed.

There is an African woman, young sexy a short skirt and hearts on her stockings.

The man of the family speaks . . .

*

A moth on the ground, it is black and grey and has decals like a vampire, is it recently out of its chrysalis?

*

. . . English, the woman only speaks Spanish. They both love their bambino, which is good. By unspoken agreement we don't speak about the Falklands war, but by its obvious absence we must both be thinking about it. They are from Buenos Aries, and they are visiting his parents for three weeks. He has brown hair blue eyes; she has blondish brown hair and blue eyes as does the bambino.

Luggage and child buggies are stowed away; the African woman goes to bed early.

To build bridges the Argentinian man and I talk about sport. Football first, I ask him if he supports the River Plate team and he says that he does. He talks about wages being four times greater in the Premier league and that most of their best players go to Europe now. I don't mention that there are few English players in the Premier league now. His main love is Rugby Union though; he complains that the best are solicitors and that they don't get enough time to practise and that black eyes and cauliflower eyes doesn't go down well with clients. Perhaps he wants his national team to be the best like their Football (soccer) team.

We settle down for the night. My bladder has a low endurance and I can't get out of the compartment. Eventually I do, but with a scolding from the African woman or maybe the Argentinian.

A few minutes later...

*

A flood of students pass they stop on the bridge in the grounds of Miramar and take photos. They are beautiful...

*

... there is an insistent knocking on the glass of the door. It is opened...

*

I cannot see them but there are fish lazily swimming on the surface of the artificial stream, just their fins show, like the tips of icebergs.

*

. . . And a fit looking Gendarme asks the African woman to get down from her couchette and out of the compartment. There is a heated discussion in French. She uses the only word I really understand 'drugs.' They ask for her luggage and . . .

*

I see the mouth of a fish, without the fear of a fishing hook, feeding on the surface.

*

. . . the gendarmes find nothing. She complains why it was only her that was searched.

The train continues through Switzerland, I glimpse some really sexy looking trains and remember some Swiss train journeys on one of the Sky channels.

I wake early and go for my breakfast in the buffet car, espresso and croissant unflavoured but heavily fulfilling.

*

. . . the sea at Mira mere is like a mirror I see it through the trees.

*

My first Italian dawn and there are clouds in the sky!
Why?

Then the sun burns some of them away. I'm surprised to see Elderflowers mixed with a flower tree growing like weeds which only reside on sheltered court yards at home. Should I get one? The sides of the railway tracks are a haven for feral trees.

There are houses with gardens that have 30 to 100 vines in them. The fallow land looks exactly the same as in England.

*

In the harbour at Grignano there is a line of children who are little more than Bambinos. I hear from the harbour Restaurant a chorus of ciao, ciao, ciao . . .

Waiting for the train

The trains in Italy are comfortable with blue plastic chairs, a lighter shade of blue marble Formica, large windows and the best bit; you can actually put your luggage in the luggage rack. The trains stay in the station for at least forty minutes, giving the cleaning crew ample time to clean the train. There is a supervisor who points out areas that require attention for cleaning and safety issues.

In Europe there is a game that they play with the tickets, you have to authenticate the ticket by pushing it into a machine, and apparently it is quite important. I joined at Trieste and forgot. To one of the cleaning crew I mimed, with a scuzzy, pushing into a machine. He mimed back, go into the station. There are no ticket barriers. The machine was very Hi tech, very shiny metal. I punched it and returned to the train, getting a very nice peach soda drink on the way.

It is hot and I'm wearing a black jacket a pair of traveling jeans and a Venetia T shirt. If I was James Bond I would say, if asked, 'I prefer to be steamed rather than fried!'

The cleaning crew makes their last checks. A man with grey hair chucks a piece of rubbish towards a waste bin hoping to save his legs a few weary steps, but misses. He has to walk, then bend down, pick it up and put it in the bin.

I see my last glimpse of Miramar it has been a very relaxing holiday, or should I say vacation, or should I say, Fiesta.

Miramar is a magical place, not a place to leave, here is heaven, it is a pinnacle of pleasantness, and no preparation for war. In war it is better to start low and rise, rather than to start high and end up low. Maximillian left here to go to Mexico and failed. The Count d'Austo left for Abyssinia, a very good commander, but we the British do not rest in beautiful places before going to war, we train in the rain. If you can live through a day of miserable cold rain, you can live through anything a human can put in your way. Leaving a beautiful place only makes your heart heavy.

*

In the castle grounds there is a sign commemorating the fact that the US army 88th division was stationed here immediately after the war until it was di-mobbed in 1947. It was involved in the start of the cold war between the West and the communist Yugoslavian regime and Soviet forces in Eastern Europe.

James Joyce stayed in Trieste town for a long time before the First World War; it was here that he wrote Ulysses and possibly Dubliners, Dubliners influences the poet Seamus Heaney, in particular the poem Bog Queen.

*

On Italian trains they speak, joke and it is a jolly affair. The air con is good on the trains as well, does this mean I will be hit by the heat in Venice?

I am in the land that invented concrete and did grand things with the material, brilliant sculptured façades; it had different grades and weights. It was impossible to build a large dome until they learnt to put the heaviest grades at the bottom, then lighten and decrease the circles until the top which was left open to increase the light going into the building. This created a strong structure that was resistant to the ravages of earth quakes, which is ironic in a way in that British Celtic houses were round and was changed to square houses. Now concrete is a flat and grey material, how far has it come?

*

I must admit that when the ticket inspector clipped my ticket he said something to me. Am I on the right train? I play the idiotic foreigner which is easy to do as my Italian is poor, and say nothing. The train goes north and it looks as if I am going to the mountains. I get slightly paranoid. There are hilly stations then I pass a river that is dried up or perhaps it is a gravel pit, it is full of trees, gravel and plant machinery to process the aggregates. The land flattens. There are flat lands now, to my mind flat lands equals the sea, so my mind quietens.

Some Americans sit opposite me and it is good to hear English again. I got talking to the Americanos; there were two women and a man. A military family, he was in the air-force, I was careful not to ask too many direct questions too early. It turned out he was a bomb disposal expert on IAD's, half German and half American. They were doing an RR tour away from the front, and were in civilian clothes. I was surprised by how calm and well-adjusted the man was. He explained that there had been a lot of research done into near explosion blasts, and brain trauma, to help soldiers. That was interesting as there can be personality changes when the brain suffers trauma and survives. I told them that I was a writer and showed them my book. He said that he admired the British army and the pioneering work that they did in bomb disposal in Northern Ireland main land England, and the blitz in World War Two.

It was all very convivial until I sensed in their voices that they were about to slip some-thing in that was controversial and they had had bad reactions to this subject before. They liked dogs, so do I, but only if someone else owns them, then they admitted that they liked Pitt Bull Terriers. Of course they received bad press; it was the owners who were at fault for their misdemeanours. I didn't mention the reports of cats and humans mauled by these lovable animals, but said that I wasn't a fan. I could of said that I preferred Artic Wolves, but didn't. The subject was dropped and the journeys of conversation and travel continued pleasantly.

It was hot when I reached Venice, and I wandered why it was always hot when I was carrying heavy bags and rainy when I just wanted to saunter around. I left my bags in the left luggage store, the guy asked for my passport and left it with him, of course I didn't understand, he had to chase me and give me back my passport. I did my traipsing around and had an excellent meal of fried chicken.

Ciao, Ciao Venice

Dreamlands Post Script

I had decided to go to Margate and the Turner Gallery after work, but writers block set in.

It was Grey in Tonbridge, and it was time for a bacon roll and coffee at the station café.

The train was fast to Ashford International. I had time for a quick espresso there. Fast to Margate, the sun burnt off any cloud here. A three bladed and solitary wind turbine at Richborough, where the cooling towers used to be, it was a solitary star burst.

Margate is welcoming, the café on the beach is open and I have a coffee.

Then I go to Tracy Em's Exhibition, to do a bit of promotion at the reception desk. I have little cash and I'm directed to the high street.

So up the concrete stairs to the Tracy Ems Exhibition, it was full of self-portraits with similar positions and different fragments of text added to them, laying bare her state of mind at that time. There was self-love and self-pain, these emotions were taken to extremes. Each work stretched the meaning of its neighbour. It was a true mood a log.

The intention was to stop at Broadstairs but I'm so into my writing that I miss my stop!

The piece I like the most is a matrass with a pruned branch on it. In the past I haven't *got* minimalist art before, but this piece said so much. It, the matrass, was used, complete with stains, but was a referral to her earlier piece 'the bed.' It was stripped bare like the blue wash nudes on the wall, no text except the bronze branch on the matrass. I ask for a title from one of the attendants, more promo work, but I say I'm beginning to get this minimalist thing. The woman says the branch represents weight I say I always chose one piece to admire she recommends a sculptural piece of a galvanised bath with a dirty Union Jack at the bottom of it, apparently Tracy is coming to terms with the aging process.

I exit, walk up to the high street, it is busy, the pier is open, there are less closed shops. I have no camera or note pad so I buy one at WH Smiths.

On the local news I hear that Dreamlands may be bought!

Dream on Margate.

Post script of the post script, Margate has been on BBC1 on the excellent 'Love actually.'

A tale of two book signings

I had a book signing in Eastbourne on Tuesday. It was held at a sea front hotel that I love. The well-practised train journey was good. It was a windy sunny day, silver rays bounced off the big waves, between St Leonards and Bexhill.

The signing was in a back room adjacent to a ball room, and a bar. There were prints on the walls, on one of the prints was a pigeon, it was like something out of a Monty Python's sketch. I followed the girl into the room. First off I chose a nice comfy settee and ordered a pot of coffee. We had agreed that I would have a long table, so I was moved to an ornate bench with a double headed eagle in the centre which hit my head.

On completion of the set up, I waited. The pigeon joined me. Landing on the tall picture rail, the room was cold. The pigeon fluffed up its feathers and shrank its head into its shoulders.

One of the compensations of being a writer is that when confronted with a situation of anxious boredom in a new place you can write, you can write about a thing that disturbs you, you can write about your surroundings.

To wit, the room had tall walls, windows and ceilings. Curtains for the windows were sashed at the side and the walls were painted pastel yellow with prints on the walls.

No one came for my books.

I ventured out into the ball room, if I was on 'strictly' I would be the buffoon, I did a few steps and gave up. There were mirrors on either ends of the walls, they were off set so the reflections spun off each other into infinity.

Half way through and I ordered my second pot of coffee. No one came. I checked my mobile for the time. I walked to the dance floor.

The pigeon occasionally flew from rail to rail, with the distinctive flapping sounds pigeons make. At one time it started preening and a white feather see-sawed down onto a writing desk.

Still no one came.

*

On Friday I went to a Soho literary festival, to perhaps sell my book and to be close to successful authors. I hadn't pre-booked so I could not get in but went to the bar and had lemonade. I recognised John Bird the comic actor and sketch master. In a corner in an enclosed booth there was a book signing going on.

I found a seat, sat down and tried to hawk my book, to a couple from Strasbourg. She was English and he was a Berliner. There was a cue at the booth, that's Michael Palin they said. I couldn't see Michael, John Bird acted like a pigeon, stood still, watched, went to the signing and returned to a lap top strewn table with attendant cables meandering about, he stood next to a rep from 'The Oldies.'

The book signing ended. Conveniently there was an external door close to the booth. It had been a long session for Michael, a two hour lecture, then the book signing and now this photo opportunity, where I got my first glimpse of Michael Palin, the professional smile was still there. He stood in the door way and allowed the rain to fall on him, they took pictures, and he smiled and was reluctantly allowed to go.

John Bird sat down and said, 'Michael's a very shy man at heart.'

Could I do that? Is that what you have to do, to endure, to sell books? I expect Michael could do with a bit of peace occasionally, that's why he travels. I would like a few of his book sales, but I know there is rarely a middle ground, that I should be glad that I have gone through the book signing with no books sold and that Michael should be glad of the sales.

Lightning Source UK Ltd.
Milton Keynes UK
UKOW051930290113

205573UK00001B/31/P